Congratulations on choosing the best in educational materials for your child. By selecting top-quality McGraw-Hill products, you can be assured that the concepts used in our books will reinforce and enhance the skills that are being taught in classrooms nationwide.

And what better way to get young readers excited than with Mercer Mayer's Little Critter, a character loved by children everywhere? Our First Readers offer simple and engaging stories about Little Critter that children can read on their own. Each level incorporates reading skills, colorful illustrations, and challenging activities.

Level 1 – The stories are simple and use repetitive language. Illustrations are highly supportive.
Level 2 - The stories begin to grow in complexity. Language is still repetitive, but it is mixed with more challenging vocabulary.
Level 3 - The stories are more complex. Sentences are longer and more varied.

To help your child make the most of this book, look at the first few pictures in the story and discuss what is happening. Ask your child to predict where the story is going. Then, once your child has read the story, have him or her review the word list and do the activities. This will reinforce vocabulary words from the story and build reading comprehension.

You are your child's first and most influential teacher. No one knows your child the way you do. Tailor your time together to reinforce a newly acquired skill or to overcome a temporary stumbling block. Praise your child's progress and ideas, take delight in his or her imagination, and most of all, enjoy your time together!

Library of Congress Cataloging-in-Publication Data

Mayer, Mercer, 1943-
My Trip to the Farm / by Mercer Mayer.
p. cm. – (First readers, skills and practice)
Summary: While visiting his grandparents at their farm, Little Critter helps by gathering the eggs, riding a horse, feeding the goats, and doing other fun jobs. Includes activities.
ISBN 1-57768-817-1
[1. Farm life—Fiction. 2. Domestic animals—Fiction. 3. Grandparents—Fiction] I. Series.

PZ7.M462 My 2001
[E]—dc21 2001026663

McGraw-Hill
Children's Publishing

A Division of The ***McGraw·Hill*** *Companies*

Send all inquiries to:
McGraw-Hill Children's Publishing
8787 Orion Place
Columbus, OH 43240-4027

Printed in the United States of America.

1-57768-817-1

1 2 3 4 5 6 7 8 9 10 PHXBK 06 05 04 03 02 01

A Big Tuna Trading Company, LLC/J. R. Sansevere Book

Level **3** Grades **1 - 2**

MY TRIP TO THE FARM

McGraw-Hill Children's Publishing

Columbus, Ohio

Last Sunday, I went to visit
my grandma and grandpa on their farm.
I had a really fun time.
I learned how to take care
of all the animals.
This is what I did.

On Monday morning,
Grandma asked me to get
some eggs from the henhouse.

I wasn't afraid of the chickens at all!

On Tuesday afternoon,
I helped Grandpa feed the goats.
I thought goats ate tin cans.
Grandpa said the goats would eat
hay and corn today.

On Wednesday night, Grandpa
showed me how to milk the cows.
Grandpa told me that cows
have a lot of extra milk.
That's why we have to milk them
in the morning and at night.

On Thursday morning,
I helped Grandma feed the pigs.
The mother pig had twelve piglets!
Grandma said that pigs have more
babies than any of the other animals
on the farm.

BUTTERCUP

On Friday afternoon, Grandpa and I
took care of the horses.
We brushed them
and cleaned their stalls.
I wanted to ride Old Kicker,
but Grandpa said Buttercup
was much more fun to ride.

On Saturday night,
Grandma cooked a big dinner.
It was my last night at the farm.
The next morning, I said good-bye
to Grandma and Grandpa.
I can't wait to come back next summer!

Word Lists

Read each word in the lists below. Then, find each word in the story. Now, make up a new sentence using the word. Say your sentence out loud.

<u>Words I Know</u>

eggs
goats
corn
milk
cows
pigs
horses

<u>Challenge Words</u>

farm
animals
henhouse
chickens
morning
night

What Did You Learn?

Circle the sentences below that tell things you learned from this story. Try not to look back at the story.

Roosters crow at the crack of dawn.

Cows need to be milked twice a day.

Sheep give us wool.

Pigs have more babies than any of the other animals on the farm.

Goats eat hay and corn.

Scarecrows keep birds away from the corn in the field.

Compound Words

A compound word is a big word made up of two smaller words put together.

Example: Henhouse is made up of hen and house.

Match words in the first column with words in the second column to make compound words. The first one has been done for you.

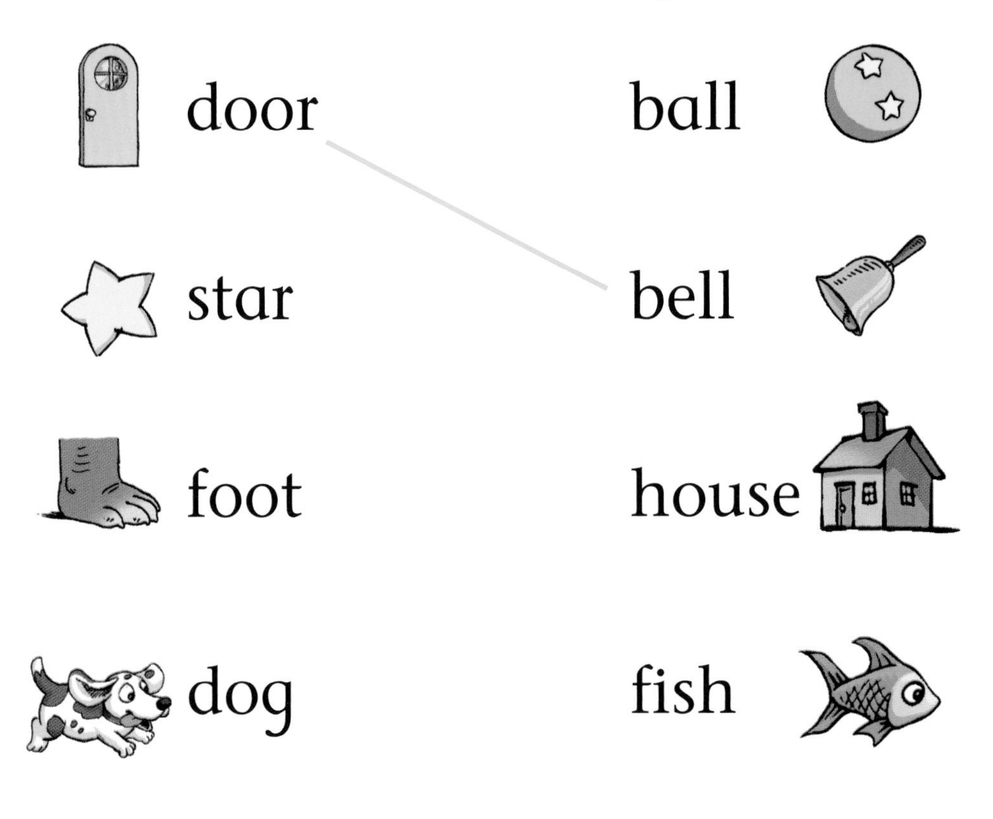

Find the two smaller words in each compound word and write them on the lines. The first one has been done for you.

snowflake = ___snow___ + ___flake___

popcorn = ____________ + ____________

handshake = ____________ + ____________

backyard = ____________ + ____________

bathtub = ____________ + ____________

pancake = ____________ + ____________

Fun with Words

Read the questions below. Write your answers on the blanks on the next page. Use the Word List below to help you.

1. In which season did Little Critter go to the farm?

2. What did the goats eat besides hay?

3. On what day did Little Critter collect eggs?

4. How many piglets did Little Critter see?

5. What time of day did Little Critter help Grandpa milk the cows?

6. Which horse did Little Critter ride?

7. On what day did Little Critter arrive at the farm?

Word List

corn	Sunday
night	Monday
twelve	summer
Buttercup	

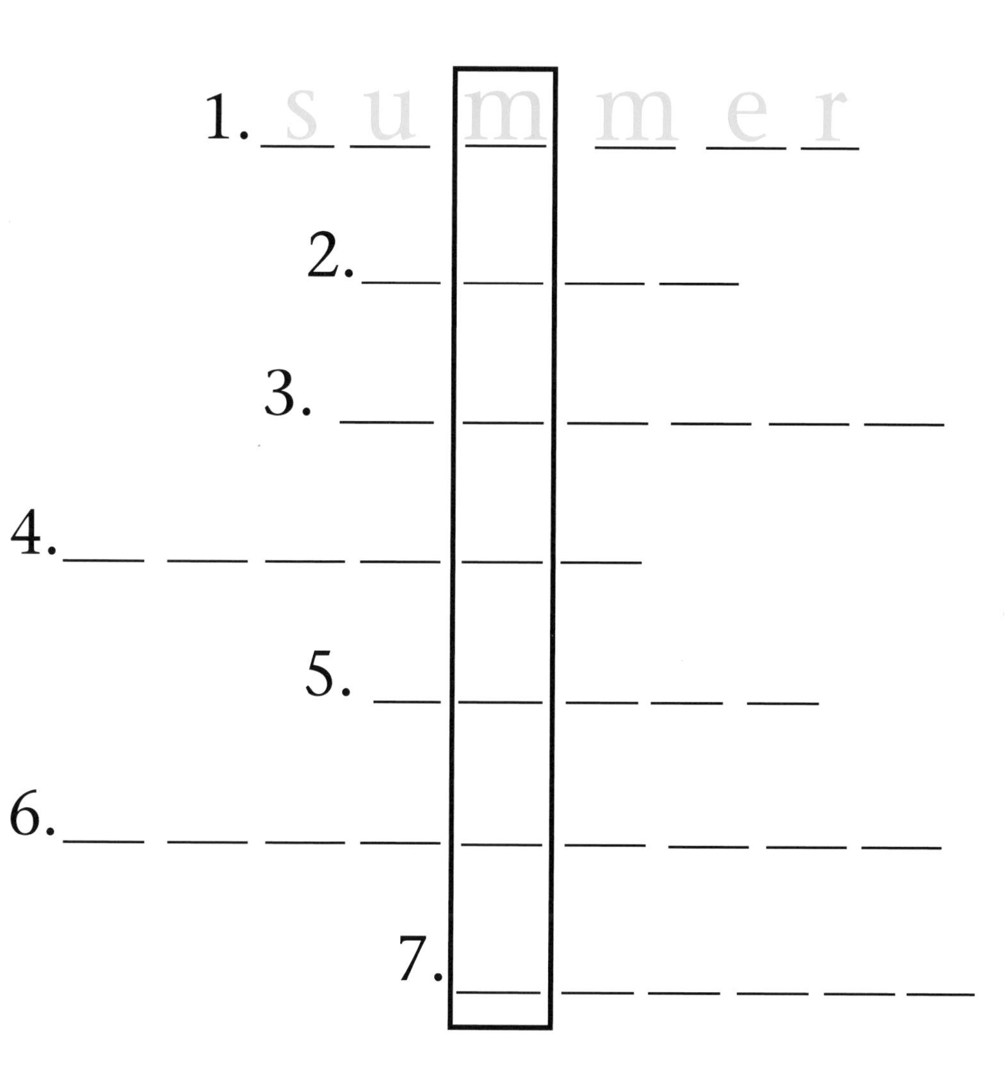

Where do cows go on Saturday night? To find out, read the letters in the box from top to bottom.

Answer Key

page 19
What Did You Learn?

Roosters crow at the crack of dawn.

Cows need to be milked twice a day.

Sheep give us wool.

Pigs have more babies than any of the other animals on the farm.

Goats eat hay and corn.

Scarecrows keep birds away from the corn in the field.

page 20
Compound Words

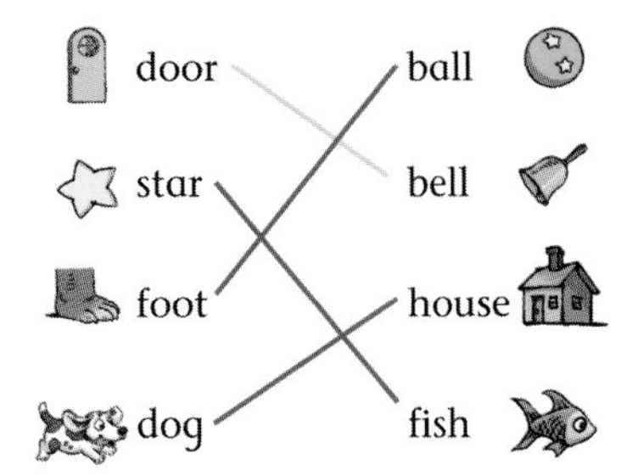

page 21
Compound Words

snowflake = snow + flake

popcorn = pop + corn

handshake = hand + shake

backyard = back + yard

bathtub = bath + tub

pancake = pan + cake

page 23
Fun with Words

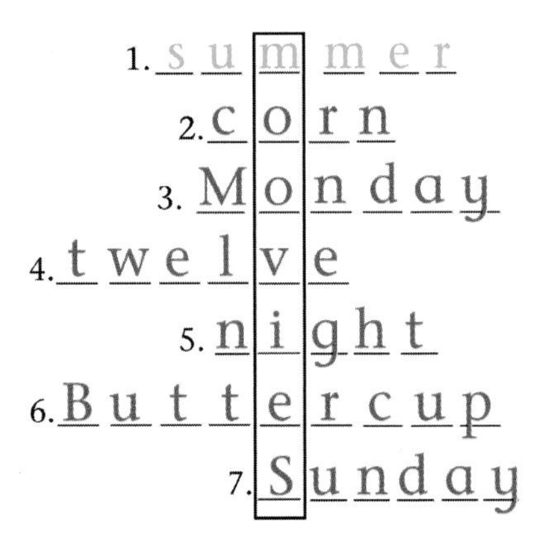